FIRST STORY

First Story's vision is a society that encourages and supports young people from all backgrounds to practise creative writing for pleasure, self-expression and agency. We believe everyone has a unique voice, a story to tell and a right to be heard. Our flagship programme places inspiring professional writers into secondary schools, where they work intensively with students and teachers to develop young people's creativity, confidence and ability. Through our core provision and extended opportunities, including competitions and events, participants develop skills to thrive in education and beyond.

Find out more at firststory.org.uk

First Story is a registered charity number 1122939 and a private company limited by guarantee incorporated in England with number 06487410. First Story is a business name of First Story Limited.

First published 2023 by First Story Limited
44 Webber Street, Southbank, London, SE1 8QW

www.firststory.org.uk

ISBN 978-0-85748-547-2

1 3 5 7 9 10 8 6 4 2

A CIP catalogue record for this book is available from the British Library.

Printed and bound in the UK by Aquatint
Typeset by Avon DataSet Ltd
Copyedited by Vivienne Heller
Proofread by Sally Beets
Cover designed by Duncan Poulton (duncanpoulton.com), based on
'Comet McNaught' by C Lindsay and 'Night sky in Freycinet, Tasmania'
by Dmitry Brant, licensed under the Creative Commons
Attribution-Share Alike 4.0 International licence:
https://creativecommons.org/licenses/by-sa/4.0/

Pieces of Us

An Anthology by the First Story Group
at Hatch End High School

EDITED BY ANTHONY ANAXAGOROU | 2023

FIRST STORY

Contents

Introduction

Anthony Anaxagorou, Writer-in-Residence

What's the purpose of poetry and why do we still need to write it? This was one of the first questions put to me by a student at Hatch End High during our first session. I'd come in to take over from a previous facilitator, so the class already had some exposure to what poetry meant or might be. As I paused to formulate an answer, I realised there wasn't really one I could honestly give. What we discussed instead was how poetry exists for its own sake, in the way a tree or a colour might. There is no quantifiable way to think of poetry or its monetary value – it holds no real currency; the people who make it tend to be either very poor or very privileged in how they can use their time. A girl asked, 'Why do you do it then?' I said that I like to work with my imagination for a living – half the group chuckled; the other half looked on, confused. But isn't that what art is? A question, some quiet laughter, contemplation, confusion, a bit of sadness – but ultimately all these aspects compound to find a way into our being, asking us to reflect on the way we live, the decisions we make and what we do with the time we have on this earth.

Over the coming weeks we looked at poems written within the last decade. We took risks with our own approaches to what we thought poetry was, and what it could be, discussing a range of pertinent issues promoted by the poems we were reading. Themes included home, the climate, social injustice, faith, hope and dreams. We found a language to articulate these ideas – we wrote with our senses; we wrote blind and around, with the aim being to rattle the reader into feeling, to comfort, surprise and astound.

Here are poems written by people at the very start of their futures. The course of their life is not yet clear. What they do know, however, is that the earth is in a bad way, humans are still hurting each other, and the same lines of inequality persist. These poems allude and gesture towards what this generation are thinking and feeling. And, for me, there is no insight more valuable.

Teacher's Foreword

Morsal Mohammad, Head of English Literature

The First Story programme has been a rewarding journey for both the teachers and the students involved. Together we explored the theme of identity and found a sense of comfort and serendipity through writing this anthology. By the end of the enlightening and rewarding programme, each student – despite their different backgrounds – had found a common ground in writing. Putting pen to paper, they understood the power of writing; they understood that their words have been their strongest tool all this time. They spent time asking questions. Who are we? What defines us? Where did we come from, and where is it that we are heading? Anthony helped the students craft both their responses to these questions and their writing skills, enabling them to stand up for the things they so strongly believe in and to write ardently about their identity, something they felt was like a shadow: not always visible to all, but always present. Anthony worked closely with the students to help their young writerly talents emerge; these have surfaced beautifully in this incredibly seamless anthology. This anthology contains our truths and hopes by showcasing the endless talents here at Hatch End High School. This anthology is an ovation to freedom, to our homes, to our loved ones, to ourselves and to peaceful coexistence.

Home

Mohammad Sajjad Farooq

The mountains, the valleys, the rivers
the wars, the deaths, the horrors
the mothers' delectable dinners
the growing number of abhorrers.

My motherland grieves over her losses
my poor, corrupted country
my motherland cries but to no avail
the graveyard of empires… Afghanistan.

Who Am I?

Aoife Rooney

The question we all ask:
Who am I?
Our names, our age, our 'ID'
are obvious answers.
But still we ask: who am I?

For we are built
and defined by too many things:
Our parents,
our history,
our friends and former friends –
they all make up the person we are now.

To choose who we are,
we have all tried to do it
but we can't, so we ask:
Who am I?

We don't want to be defined
by those around us.
So we try to break free
of it all by asking ourselves:
Who am I?

But I want to ask you
who do you want to be?
Not who are you
but what do *you* do
and think about to make you
you?

Her

Marwa Moslemi

How are they
over there
all the way
in Afghanistan?
She's walking
scared trying
to shield her
sensitive skeleton
from the ill
fireworks.
She just needed
some water
but instead
received beige
confetti
in her eyes,
nose,
mouth.
Forced to do
things against
her will,
married at seven
chef at eight
mother at fifteen.
Help these girls
before it's too late.

Uncle

Marwa Moslemi

We're all humans:
we live, we die.
All of us laugh,
cry. It's all nature,
that's the truth,
but things aren't easy,
it all starts with youth.

We get older,
the world gets colder,
we all need a shoulder
to lean on. Some of us live
some die, some get cancer
and some of us lie.

He's gone because of nature,
painful excruciating nature
that he had to live through.
Mother was crying. He was dying.
Now he's gone.

And on an empty canvas,
tears are drawn.

To my late uncle Mukhtar Majid.
Brother, father, uncle, artist.
I Love You.

How Can I Define Myself?

Sara Mohamedova

'How do you define yourself?'
A question with no definite answer
one that confuses the brain
forcing you to probe deeper
into your own mind to delve
the workings of yourself.

'How do you define yourself?'

I'll start from the beginning
from my first years alive
then I'll go from the present
describing myself now.

Shall I tell you of my culture
and heritage? How can some adjectives
and an anecdote encompass who I am?

All of this begs the question,
'How do *you* define *yourself?*'

Emotions…

Sara Mohamedova

… are things that show your humanity
that control your actions,

emotions are the truest things
powerful tools to enhance the mind,

they dictate your rationality
they can make or break you,

emotions are made to be expressed
and felt.

A Look into My Book

Edwyn Boateng

With the blood of a refined warrior,
From the planet of independence.
I'm a lion rushing down with unbelievable force.
My influence will inspire even bugs to become giants.
Life's too short to be thinking about the negatives.
I'll spend all of mine making memories and differences.

My land is precious and the culture rich,
the streets may be messy but I love it.
Not a single speck of silence seen during the day.
Once you taste the art your mouth will be suicidal.
Good luck napping in this country of gold.

Am I Wrong Though?

Edwyn Boateng

It's not called being down bad,
it's just appreciating the gifts
you have witnessed.

It's called loving someone
for what they are and not
being afraid to hide it.

Next time you call someone
down bad, take it back and think.
They are just expressing their opinion –

an act of kindness.

Creativity

Pawel Lukasik

School is like prison,
same repetitive routine,
same scheduled food,
same old group of friends,
same set of rules.

However, you can be creative,
whether it's in maths class,
or during physics – something
can always be found.

Sitting on a chair,
playing with your hair,
at some point, staring out
the window is fair, other days
it's better to be drawn.

Untitled

Elijah Makusha

London feels like home
Because of the family that lives here,
Of the friends that I have made here
And it is the place where I have adapted

Because of the chilly winter days
where I can stay in blankets the entire day,
of the rain where I stay home and play,
of the feeling when you're walking with walkers

Always and Forever

Safa Osman

Land of sea
peace and tranquillity
hopefully there will be
in the horn of Africa
where we live as community.

Here we laugh and cry
this land is our home
always and more
Somalia – Africa's treasure

Blood, Sweat and Tears

Safa Osman

Where guns lie
lives come and go,
people die
knowing they won't go home.

Blood, sweat and tears,
nothing but the constant ringing
in our ears. Peace is the enemy
that is never civil –
it is as if their lives aren't beneficial,
going at the crack of dawn,
coming back is a promise
never sworn.

Cautious Soul

Aliza Adams

I am a homebody
a cautious soul.
Somedays I am a stray star
hidden deep in the abyss,
other days I feel like the sun.
Bold. Daring. Illuminate.

The Girl with No Face

Aliza Adams

Envy follows them home
stalks their dreams
scrolling through the overvalued
piece of metal as they slowly drown,
being consumed, engulfed, and taken
by envy.

Envy has no face
no soul, no body –
an overbearing spirit,
an ominous presence
that plagues them.

Envy lurks in the mind
of the innocent: the emerald
green aura overpowers
the pure, loving, and carefree
state of being.

Envy does not want to invoke
this pain, this cruelty
but it's her job, her fate…

Take My Family out of the Cold

Olivia Milner

The constant rain and clouds
boring city views
and you just want something new.
I want to be where it's sunny
but I need to get the money
and this is the only place I can get it
this busy city with multiple opportunities.
I love seeing my family
take us somewhere hot
and it'll never get old.
Take me home?

Smiles and Happy Energy

Olivia Milner

I'm really chill,
I'm the best in the family
because I'm rarely ill.
My childhood was pretty different,
anger, sadness and negativity.
What happened to the smiles
and happy energy? My dad
wasn't very persistent,
would come and go.

This is the type of life
I lived but now it's the same
every morning.
I'm always tired,
never much energy.
I go home to sleep
Even if it's just a second.

Motherland

Heena Babar

What do I know about my motherland?
Afghanistan is a beautiful place,
from the food to the cloth.
How I wish I could visit,
without being hurt,
with the cloth full of colour,
and the flavours of spicy food,
all the sweets that would make
your mouth water.

Sadness

Heena Babar

Sadness
the way you feel
when something bad happens;
the way your heart drops from pain,
how you wish you could chance something
that is unchangeable,
that's the feeling of sadness,
when someone you loved
lets go!

Iraq

Amna Beigzie

Iraq, a place full of spark,
somewhere that will always leave a mark
deep down in my heart.
The food always lightens the mood,
the heat would want to make you take a seat.

People will charge at you like an eagle,
dangerous streets
where most people meet.
The crowded shops,
never surrounded by cops.
That's Iraq, but the spark
will always remain in my heart.

Misfits

Piotr Lukasik

> Being not in the conversation,
> Being irrelevant to others,
> Makes me feel a weird feeling,
> Makes me feel sorry for myself,
> It's not good to feel like this, loneliness,
> It may not always be bad though,
> Sometimes it doesn't show,
> Sometimes it's better to be alone.

Out of Control

Piotr Lukasik

It feels like someone else is in control,
like whatever I do I'll be criticised,
do this, do that,
     you are doing it wrong,
as if I have no right.

What if you had no choices?

Peace

Malak Sharif

Peace is quiet
the sound of rain
breathing fresh air
the feeling of freedom.

Not having stress around you
when everything is okay
when you aren't disturbed
when you're healthy.

We all want this –
to tuck our legs in our blanket
to not have people near
to have some time to ourselves.

Power Hungry

Oytun Yalcin

Taking over,
one by one,
day after day,
the deed will be done.

Consuming strength,
eating it up,
destroying land,
leaving not even a flower,
because you're a tyrant,
only hungry for power.

I Am or Am I?

Oytun Yalcin

I am a child
just trying to fit in,
just trying to find myself,
so I'll have to search within.

Am I who I'm supposed to be?
The answer to that,
I am trying to see.
Every day I think and think,
who am I? What is my identity?

Something Is There

Huda Hiis

The walls grab me
They feel my emotion
My heart breathes
It feels my corrosion

My lungs pop
   They feel the explosion
      The vines are growing
     They're reaching
        They're breathing

           I am not what I think
            Time is gone
             Gone is Time
              What am I?

It Will Go Away Soon

Huda Hiis

My mouth blinks
　My eyes stutter
　　I don't see it
　　　I don't hear it
　　　I taste it
　　　　I hate it
　　　　　I hate it?
　　　　　I love it?
　　　　　　I love… it?

I Am Krish

Krish Krishnapillai

Seen many countries but want to visit more,

Ate all kinds of food but want to try more,

Met many people but want to meet more,

Seen a lot of money but want to make more,

Played many games but want to play more,

Laughed for hours but want to laugh more,

Achieved many goals but want to reach the rest.

My Home Country

Krish Krishnapillai

The palm trees, the houses, the beaches
my home country,

the pollution, the corruption, the overheat
my home country,

the language, the food, the people
my home country,

the wars, the racism, the crime
my home country,

the friendship, the family, the love
my home country, Sri Lanka.

Home Country

Farhan Younusi

Mountains and rivers as rich as gold
yet the people have yet to have a meal.

Rivers and valleys gushing with gold
but the people are yet to flourish.

The lack of wealth finds richness
in other ways.

The sound of community, the love
and kindness is worth a tonne.

People make the country rich
humble Afghanistan.

Identity

Farhan Younusi

I am Farhan,
the one who tries his best
and hardest. The world weighs
on my shoulders. It is the simplest
of things that feel the toughest.

Praying, being good and staying positive.
I try to remain a humble child.

War

Reda Alawad

The sadness watching my country fall,
seeing everyone depressed but standing tall,
the other country, rise to power,
while families in our country lay down flowers,
the traumatising feeling you get
is something you can never forget.

They say I'm a terrorist,
making me consider if I need a therapist,
I'm just a thirteen-year-old boy
trying to live life and enjoy.

Serendipity

Morsal Mohammad

Home.
 Fresh bread
 Morning laughter
 Green tea
 Grape vines.

Home.
 Starry skies
 Mountain views
 Mud huts
 Busy bazaars.

Home.
 School girls
 White scarves
 Tattered shoes
 Hopeful smiles.

Home.
 Fierce women
 Leonine men
 Wise elders.

Home.
 Mothers' love
 Fathers' protection
 A child's haven.

Home.
    Not the West's playground
    Not a no man's land
    Not a toy.

Home.
    Our Identity.
    Our Pride.
    Our Solace.
    Our Paradise.
    Our Home.

Letters from Me to You

Morsal Mohammad

I sit here in awe,
    in awe of you and where you belong.
I sit here in awe,
    in awe of the world you are now in.

You are the sky above
    and I am the ocean beneath.
You light up the stars
    and I reflect them in my reefs.

Darkness meets the dusk,
    dusk meets the blues.
The blues and pinks meet like a hug from me to you.

Not very often I get to write to you so close
even though we are seven skies apart
    you will always be near.
These silver linings prove you too are here.

I sit here in awe,
    in awe of the world you are now in.

The Pathologist's Knife

Shoshana Rothstein

Another cadaver, another person that was
two lungs. Two kidneys. A liver. A heart.
The same chance arrangement of tissues and cells.
The same arrangement after death.
The pathologist's knife salivates equally over all.

Powerful Enough

Shoshana Rothstein

The white paper waits beneath my pen,
a snowy vast expanse beyond limits
except those imposed by the weight of language
that cuts into the soft impossibility of what I want to express.

The words rage and ravage against the page,
tight-lipped, foaming like whitened waves,
frustrated into wind-whipped anger,
powerful. But not powerful enough.

What I want to express, calm and patient, resists.
Like a tired parent, it sighs,
exasperated.
It knows that these words
cannot win.

And so, confined by borders,
my words remain. Fated to spend
forever trying and yearning and faulty
when they want to be conquering.
Ferociously.

BIOGRAPHIES

ALIZA ADAMS was born during the falling of vibrant coloured leaves – red, orange and golden – on 1st October. Her fourteen-year-old mind loves watching *Marvel*, the deep story of connected movies, and watching the heat of enemies burn into passionate lovers. The melodic voice of music soft tumbles her eyes closed as the dim light of her phone shines with the photogenic boards of Pinterest. Her character is that of a bright and warm-hearted girl who holds the care of people, who she calls her 'lovelies', deep in her branches of thoughts and loving memories.

REDA ALAWAD is in Year 9 and enjoys sports, gaming and watching Liverpool play.

HEENA BABAR is a thirteen-year-old poet who is from Afghanistan, born in England. Her favourite colour is red because she says that it's a nice colour. She is very excited to have been a part of a published book, because she is proud. She is hyped because it is a big achievement.

AMNA BEIGZIE is a fourteen-year-old who enjoys cooking, baking and shopping.

MR EDWYN BOATENG is a bright young man who is currently at the ripe young age of fourteen. He has high aspirations whilst also being an extremely hardworking gentleman. He believes that he can change the world step by step. He enjoys researching public figures and exercising daily, which is quite unusual for his age. He is fond of basketball and even track and field. In the future, he wants to become a star athlete to inspire young people just like him to come out of their comfort zone.

MOHAMMAD SAJJAD FAROOQ is a young man who is fourteen years old, his favourite subject is Maths, and he wants to become an engineer in the future. He loves reading and his favourite book is *Alex Rider*. His strongest point of English is poetry. He is known as a caring, smart and respected young man who has a bright future ahead of him. Sajjad is overly ambitious about his goals and is willing to work as hard as he can to reach them.

HUDA HIIS is a bright, imaginative and capable young girl with a creative mind and powerful mindset. Huda enjoys a variety of different hobbies; her favourite pastime is getting lost in the vivid word of video games, particularly ones with a detailed plotline. She also has high ambitions for the future, planning on becoming an established dermatologist, further showcasing her selfless and empathetic traits. Despite her bubbly, kind personality, Huda deeply values her alone time with her thoughts. She adores many different types of scenery, especially the beach, describing it as her sanctuary.

KRISH KRISHNAPILLAI is fourteen years old. He is popular among his friends as he is full of knowledge and humour. He holds *Avengers: Infinity War* close to his heart since it reminds him of the hype surrounding its release. He likes fame because he would prefer for his works to blow up in popularity while he is alive rather than after he is dead. He also draws as his hobby, especially graffiti. He practises printing names in graffiti form in his spare time to improve. Krish loves socialising and is always optimistic.

PAWEL LUKASIK is in Year 9 and enjoys Maths and Computer Science.

PIOTR LUKASIK was born in England with Polish heritage. He is in Year 9 and enjoys Computer Science. He hopes to develop the best game the world has known. He believes all dreams are achievable, especially with hard work and determination.

ELIJAH MAKUSHA is in Year 9. He likes going out and being with his friends.

OLIVIA MILNER is a fourteen-year-old student at Hatch End High School. She likes listening to music and doing special-effects makeup in her spare time.

SARA MOHAMEDOVA is an ambitious, young and spirit-filled homebody who thoroughly enjoys the art of video games, especially *Roblox*. Her birthday falls in the summer, on 17th June, which contradicts her adoration for autumn. Sara sees herself with a stable career thriving in a prestigious law firm. Her competitive nature, however, does not collide with her love for nature-filled scenery. Sara is infatuated with the beauty of rainforests, while also being captivated and consumed by poetry. We can all clearly see her passion for literature in her works of art as a poet.

MARWA MOSLEMI is a young, thirteen-year-old girl. Her hobbies consist of martial arts, drawing, swimming and poetry. She is from Afghanistan, but she was born here. She says that she has been inspired to do this so that she can express her feelings. She has no favourite colour as she does not like being biased. She says that she can't wait to see her poem in a book!

SAFA OSMAN is a fourteen-year-old. She aspires to become a paediatrician one day. As a child, her favourite author was Jacqueline Wilson; however, over the years, she has taken a keen interest in biographies and thrilling short stories.

AOIFE ROONEY loves to read any book she can get her hands on. She also enjoys playing the piano and participating in ballet.

MALAK SHARIF is a fourteen-year-old who likes to watch movies.

OYTUN YALCIN is a thirteen-year-old young, aspiring poet with an amazing future ahead of him. Oytun is an amazing person who is kind, genuine and an intellectual poet with deep thinking skills. Coming from the school Hatch End, he will definitely be a prodigy in poetry. He comes from Turkey and is ethnically Kurdish. He enjoys reading sci-fi and loves basketball.

FARHAN YOUNUSI is a thirteen-year-old boy from Northwest London. He is ethnically from Afghanistan. His hobbies consist of gaming, basketball and acting. He is an aspiring young poet with a bright future ahead of him. He is (at the time of writing) a Year 9 student at Hatch End High School. He is described by members of staff as a very polite young man, and is expected to win many awards during his time at Hatch End. He is a young prodigy and is an up-and-coming underdog in the First Story programme. It is predicted that his poetry mindset will expand due to his above-average IQ for his age. This makes him an unmatched beast in the world of poetry due to his intellectual knowledge and passion, driving him to improve and be the best he can be.

SHOSHANA ROTHSTEIN is a Jewish female English teacher. Born and raised in London as the oldest of four sisters, she has always loved reading and writing.

MORSAL MOHAMMAD is a female Afghan teacher. Born and raised in Copenhagen, Denmark, Morsal moved to London with her family when she was ten. As the years went on, she found her passion and love for literature ever-growing. She studied English Literature and Creative Writing followed by a PGCE. She visited her motherland, Afghanistan, for the first time in twenty-one years and instantly felt a deep-rooted connection. Upon her arrival, she wrote and illustrated comics related to her motherland. Morsal has now been working as an English teacher for more than six years and enjoys raising the next generation of confident writers. It goes without saying she is ever so proud of the army of poets that has created this anthology. She sends her special thanks to Anthony – a gem in the poetry world.

ACKNOWLEDGEMENTS

Melanie Curtis at Avon DataSet for her overwhelming support for First Story and for giving her time in typesetting this anthology.

Vivienne Heller for copy-editing and Sally Beets for proofreading this anthology.

Duncan Poulton for designing the cover of this anthology.

Foysal Ali at Aquatint for printing this anthology at a discounted rate.

The Founders of First Story:
Katie Waldegrave and William Fiennes.

The Trustees of First Story:
Ed Baden-Powell (chair), Aziz Bawany, Aslan Byrne, Sophie Harrison, Sue Horner, Sarah Marshall, Bobby Nayyar, Jamie Waldegrave and Ella White.

First Story Ambassadors:
Patrice Lawrence MBE and Tracy Chevalier FRSL.

Thanks to our funders:
Jane & Peter Aitken, Amazon Literary Partnership, Authors' Licensing and Collecting Society (ALCS), Arts Council England, Tim Bevan & Amy Gadney, Fiona Byrd, The Blue Thread, Boots Charitable Trust, Fiona Byrd, Full House Literary Magazine, Garfield Weston Foundation, Goldsmith's Company Charity, John Lyons Charity, John R Murray Charitable Trust, Man Charitable Trust, Mercers' Company Charity, Paul Hamlyn Foundation, family and friends of Philip Pyke, ProWritingAid, RWHA Charity Fund, teamArchie, Wellington Management UK Foundation, Wordbank, the Friends of First Story and our regular supporters, individual donors and those who choose to remain anonymous.

Pro bono supporters and delivery partners including:
Arvon Foundation, BBC Teach, British Library, Cambridge University, Centre for Literacy in Primary Education, David Higham Associates, Driver Youth Trust, English and Media Centre, Forward Arts Foundation, Greenwich University, Hachette, Hull University, Huddersfield University, National Literacy Trust, Nottingham Trent University, Penguin Random House and Walker Books.

Most importantly we would like to thank the students, teachers and writers who have worked so hard to make First Story a success this year, as well as the many individuals and organisations (including those who we may have omitted to name) who have given their generous time, support and advice.